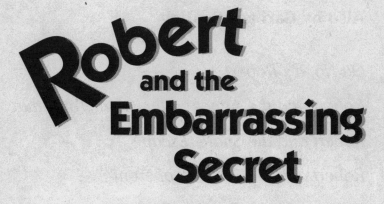

Robert
and the
Embarrassing
Secret

Also by Barbara Seuling

Robert
and the
Embarrassing
Secret

by Barbara Seuling
Illustrated by Paul Brewer

A
LITTLE APPLE
PAPERBACK

SCHOLASTIC INC.

New York Toronto London Auckland Sydney
Mexico City New Delhi Hong Kong Buenos Aires

ISBN 0-439-44378-4

All rights reserved. Published by Scholastic Inc., 557 Broadway, New York, NY 10012, by arrangement with Carus Publishing Company. SCHOLASTIC and associated logos are trademarks and/or registered trademarks of Scholastic Inc.

12 11 10 9 8 7 6 5 4 3 2 1   3 4 5 6 7 8/0

Printed in the U.S.A.   40
First Scholastic printing, September 2003

Contents

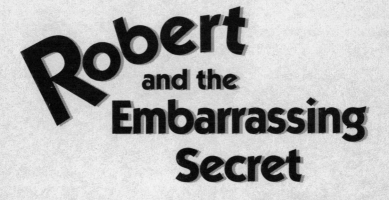

Robert and the Embarrassing Secret

The Clouded Leopard

"**M**om! Mom!" Robert burst into the house like a small explosion.

Huckleberry ran on his fat little puppy legs to greet him. Robert scooped up the wiggly dog and nuzzled him as he looked around. "Where's Mom, Huck?"

Robert's mom came dashing down the stairs. "What's wrong?" she asked.

Robert put Huckleberry down. The puppy started chewing on his shoelaces.

"Nothing's wrong," said Robert. "I just got picked to be a clouded leopard!"

1

"Slow down, Robert," said Mrs. Dorfman. "What's a clouded leopard? And why were you picked to be one?"

Robert pulled his foot gently from Huckleberry's grasp. He slipped his backpack off and opened the zipper.

"It's this," he said, pulling out a picture. He showed it to his mom. "It's a leopard with these amazing spots that look like little clouds," said Robert. "Everyone gets to be an endangered animal and has to do a report on it. I want to dress up as one. Can you make me a costume to look like this, Mom?" Robert took a second to breathe. "Can you?"

Mrs. Dorfman seemed to swallow hard. "I . . . I . . . Can't we buy one?" she said.

Robert knew they would never find a clouded leopard costume. He'd have to think of something else.

"That's okay, Mom. Never mind." He got up to go, grabbing his backpack. He motioned for Huckleberry to follow.

"Wouldn't you like a glass of milk or juice?" asked his mom.

"No, thanks," said Robert, running up the stairs. Huckleberry bumbled along beside him. "I have to get started on my homework."

Robert's room was cluttered with all his hobbies. First there were his animals.

He had his turtledoves, Flo and Billie, in a birdcage on his bookcase.

Beside the birdcage was a plastic case that contained a huge hairy tarantula named Fuzzy.

Next to his bed there was a soft bed for Huckleberry. The puppy never slept in his dog bed because he slept with Robert, but it was there, just in case. It was filled with dog toys.

Then there were Robert's collections.

Robert had a row of Weird & Wacky Facts books on his bookshelf.

He had rocks from every place he or his family had ever been.

He had jelly jars with interesting things he'd found in Van Saun Park. One was a tiny G.I. Joe combat boot. Some kid must have lost it by the duck pond.

And he had his plastic dinosaurs, lined up according to size on the windowsill.

In the center of Robert's room was his beanbag chair. He sat in it to think. Sometimes his best friend, Paul, sat in it with him when they had to think together.

Robert lifted Huckleberry and sat in the beanbag chair with him. "I want to do something special for my report," he told the puppy. The cuddly puppy sniffed at Robert's ear.

"A costume would have been great." Robert sighed. "What else can I do?" Huckleberry licked Robert's cheek. Laughing, Robert held up his hands in front of his face and peeked through his fingers. "Hey, great idea, Huck!" he exclaimed. "I'll make a mask!"

"Paper Mashay"

Thumping downstairs with Huckleberry at his heels, Robert went to the kitchen cabinet and took out a mixing bowl. Then he went to the flour canister and scooped some flour into the bowl.

Ms. Valentine, the art teacher, had showed Robert's class how to make masks with something called "paper mashay." Except she pronounced it funny, like "pop-ee-ay mashay."

Carefully, Robert climbed the stairs carrying the bowl of flour. "Don't trip me,

Huckleberry," he said. In the bathroom, he poured water over the flour until it got sticky and gooey. In his room again, he put the bowl on his desk.

He needed lots of newspaper. He and Huckleberry thumped downstairs again.

He had almost all of last Sunday's Star-Ledger in his arms when his dad came in.

"Hi, Tiger," he said. "How's it going?"

Robert's father often called him "Tiger." Robert thought it was because his dad wished Robert were more of an athlete, like his brother, Charlie.

"Hi, Dad. Fine," he said.

"What are the newspapers for?"

"A mask," said Robert.

"He's going to be a clouded leopard," said his mom, coming out of the kitchen with a steaming mug of tea in her hand.

While his mom explained to his dad what a clouded leopard was, Robert and

Huckleberry thundered back upstairs.

Robert looked at the picture. First, he needed a round shape. A soccer ball would be good, but he didn't have a soccer ball. Charlie had a basketball. Maybe he could borrow it. No, he'd better not even ask.

He looked under his bed. There was a lego piece, a sock, a chew toy and—just what he needed—a balloon he had never blown up.

Robert blew up the balloon and made a knot in it. Huckleberry watched, his tail wagging. "This isn't for you, Huckleberry," he told the puppy. He handed Huckleberry a squeaky chew toy from the dog bed instead.

He spread out some of the newspaper on the floor and cut strips from the rest. He soaked the strips in the bowl with the flour paste mixture.

When the paper was good and wet, he laid it across one side of the balloon and

smoothed it out. He waited for the strips
to dry, touching them every few minutes.
In between he played with Huckleberry.

He did several layers. They took a long
time to dry. Finally, he decided to start his

homework so he could stop fussing with the wet strips. The squeaks from Huckleberry's toy, as he played with it, made Robert smile.

When his mom called him to dinner, Robert checked the mask. It was still wet. Huckleberry had fallen asleep, his chew toy next to him. Robert tiptoed out of the room, letting him sleep. He would be back later to finish up. He washed his hands in the bathroom and went downstairs to dinner.

Protectors of the Earth

They sat around the dinner table while his mom filled their plates from the big pot. On Robert's plate she put one large lump and two small ones, covered with gravy.

"Well, Tiger, what about this project of yours?" asked his dad.

"We have to study about endangered animals," said Robert. "Mrs. Bernthal says it's our job to protect the earth and all its creatures."

"What do you have to learn about these animals?" his dad asked.

"About how they live, I guess." Robert stabbed the large brown lump with his fork.

"And how they die!" added Charlie.

Robert didn't think that was funny, even though it was true.

"Charlie . . ." said Mrs. Dorfman.

"It's true, Mom," said Charlie. "Elephants, rhinos . . . lots of animals die because people want their tusks or horns. I saw it on TV. They even club baby seals to death just to get their fur!"

Robert felt his stomach flip. "They do not!" he protested. Charlie was always teasing him. This sounded like another of his teases. He looked at his dad for him to agree. But his dad didn't say anything.

"Oh," said his mom, "I have good news! Your grandmother is coming to visit."

Robert was grateful to his mom for changing the subject. She knew how he felt about animals. He tried to cut the lump on his fork with his knife.

"Really?" said Charlie. "When?

"On Friday," said Mrs. Dorfman. "She'll be here when you get home from school."

Robert loved Grandma Judy. It's true she smoked too much. His father wrinkled his nose whenever she lit up a cigarette, so she went outside in the yard to smoke. But Grandma Judy made them laugh and she always brought presents for him and Charlie.

Robert's knife slid off the lump as he sawed away and splashed gravy across the table. "Oops!" he said.

"That knife must be dull," said his mom, jumping up. She got a wet cloth and wiped the table.

Robert pushed the lump off his fork and ate the smaller one instead. What was it— a potato? He had no idea.

Last time Grandma Judy visited, she brought Robert a glow-in-the-dark poster of Jurassic Park because she knew he liked dinosaurs. It was so terrifying, he couldn't sleep, so he rolled it up and put it in his closet. He would have to take it out and put it up when Grandma Judy was here. He didn't want to hurt her feelings. He would just have to remember not to look at the poster before he went to bed at night.

After dinner, Robert ran upstairs to finish his mask.

"Oh, no!" he cried as he went into his room. The bowl with the flour paste mixture was upside down, and Huckleberry was licking the paste off the newspapers. Robert grabbed the puppy and ran downstairs.

"Mom! Dad! Huckleberry ate my paper mashay!" he cried. "He's poisoned!"

"It was just flour and water, right?" asked his mom.

Robert nodded, his heart beating rapidly.

"He may have a bellyache," said his dad, "but he'll be okay. You're going to have to be more careful, Tiger. Puppies think everything is food."

Robert kept an eye on Huckleberry as he cleaned up the mess. That was a close call. He didn't know what he'd do if anything happened to his puppy.

His mask seemed to be okay. Robert felt it. It was still damp, but he could finish it tomorrow. He put it up high on his dresser so Huckleberry couldn't reach it.

As he got ready for bed, Robert thought again about what Charlie had said. He squeezed toothpaste onto his toothbrush. As he brushed, Robert couldn't help thinking about those baby seals. He spat into the sink.

He remembered a report he once did on sea turtles. They swallowed plastic bags that floated in the water, thinking they were food. Many of them died. Maybe every animal was in danger of something. And maybe he could figure out a way to help them.

Auntie Fur

At Paul's house after school, Robert and Paul did their homework together.

Robert sat at Paul's computer, clicking on website after website. He found out a lot of animals were in danger. They were hunted for their tusks or horns or fur—not even for food.

"Look at this!" he cried out. Paul rolled off the bed and came over to see. It was a website about hunting baby seals. A series of photos showed the friendly seals coming up to greet the hunters, who then clubbed them to death.

Paul looked on, horrified.

"I thought Charlie was teasing me," said Robert. "But it's true!"

They continued to read together.

Robert pulled up a page on the clouded leopard. It showed the spots that looked like little clouds.

"It's beautiful," said Paul.

"Yeah," said Robert. "But it says here it's being hunted for it unusual fur." Robert printed out the page.

"Did you see *101 Dalmatians*?" he asked Paul.

"Yeah!" said Paul. "Cruella De Vil—she was scary—wanted to make a coat out of those little puppies. That was a great movie."

"Yeah," Robert agreed sadly, moving aside to give Paul a turn.

Paul clicked away.

"There's a group called Greenpeace," he said. "They go in boats and stop the hunters."

"Really?" said Robert. "That's cool."

"Yeah," agreed Paul.

"Here's something about an anti-fur group."

"Who's Auntie Fur?" asked Robert.

"It's not a person," said Paul, laughing. "It's a group. They are against killing animals for their fur."

"We should do what they do," said Robert.

"I don't think so," said Paul. "They spray paint fur coats whenever they see them—even when they're on people!"

"No!" said Robert. "I wouldn't do that. Besides, my parents would kill me."

"But look! It says they also carry signs outside stores that sell fur," added Paul, still looking at the computer screen.

"We could do that," said Robert. "The signs would tell people why it's wrong to wear fur coats. Then they won't go in and buy them. We can ask some kids in our class to do it with us."

"Won't we get in trouble?" asked Paul

"I don't know," said Robert. "But we have to do something to save these animals!"

That night, Robert woke up in a terrible fright. He had been dreaming. Cruella De Vil was running after Huckleberry, waving a knife. Huck kept tumbling and falling and Cruella was getting closer and closer to him.

Robert went back to sleep with Huckleberry wrapped in his arms.

Bingo!

By three o'clock on Friday, the whole class had heard about the anti-fur protest and wanted to be part of it. The plan was set.

A week from tomorrow, on Saturday morning, they would meet at the mall. They would make signs to carry telling people why they shouldn't buy fur coats. They would carry their signs as they marched up and down in front of Fancy Furs, a store. As the bell rang, they were still talking about it.

When Robert opened the door to his house, he knew Grandma Judy was there. He smelled her perfume. It was like a flower garden.

"Is that my sweet Robert?" he heard from the kitchen. He ran in, dropping his backpack behind him.

"Grandma Judy!" he cried, wrapping his arms around her as far as they would go. His mom smiled from across the table.

Grandma Judy smothered him with kisses. "How are you?" she asked. "You have grown so tall since I last saw you, I hardly recognized you." Grandma Judy always said that.

Huckleberry tried to scramble up Robert's pants leg. "I'm fine," said Robert, picking up the puppy and holding him up. "Look, Grandma Judy, I got a puppy! His name is Huckleberry."

"Well, it's about time," Grandma Judy said, winking at Robert's mom. She reached into a big canvas bag next to her chair and took out a hard rubber bone. "The man at the store said this would be good for a puppy's teeth," she said, giving it to him. "So hello, Huckleberry."

Robert put Huckleberry down to play with his new bone. How did Grandma Judy know to bring his dog a toy?

"Your mother told me about your dog," Grandma Judy said. It was like she could read his mind.

Charlie came in. "Hi, Grandma Judy." He kissed her, and Grandma Judy grabbed him in a big hug and kissed him back.

"Look how you've grown!" she said. "These boys are going to be taller than me, soon."

"Mom," said Robert's mother, "Charlie has been taller than you for two years already. Stand up. You'll see how tall he is."

"Never mind," said Grandma Judy. "I'll see soon enough." Grandma Judy was really short, but she did not like to be teased about it.

Then she grabbed the handles on the canvas bag, lifted it up, and dumped it out on the table.

Among the hairbrush, lipstick, pack of cigarettes, book of matches, wallet, little pocket pack of tissues, small black address book, ball of green wool, crochet needle, keys, several hard candies, a magazine, two pens, and Grandma Judy's lucky charm—a plastic monkey that Robert had given her when he was five years old—was money. Lots and lots of money.

"Wow!" was all Robert could say.

"This is from bingo," she said. "I've been having a lucky streak."

Mom laughed. "It couldn't be because you buy ten cards at once, could it?"

Robert had heard about Grandma Judy playing bingo every week at the senior center. He had no idea she played for money.

"I have no idea how much is there," she said. "You and Charlie get to count it—then you and Charlie get to keep it." Immediately, the boys scrambled for the

money. At the sudden movement, Huck-leberry came running to see what was going on.

"You'll split it fifty-fifty, of course," she added. They slowed down.

Robert started to count, but Charlie was faster, so he let his brother do it. While Charlie counted it a second time, to be sure, Robert reached for Huckleberry's ball and rolled it for him. The puppy bounced after it.

Charlie made piles of ten-, five-, and one-dollar bills, plus three stacks of quarters.

"There's one hundred and seventy-six dollars, Grandma Judy," Charlie said.

"Wonderful," she said. "Now you are rich men."

Robert's mom laughed. "That's a lot of money," she said. "Maybe you should put it away for something special."

"I know something special I'm going to buy with my money," Charlie announced.

"What's that?" asked his mother.

"A new skateboard," he said. "I saw it at the sports store. It glows in the dark."

"You don't go skateboarding at night," his mom reminded him.

"I know, but I think it's neat," Charlie said.

Robert was still trying to figure out how much money each of them would get. He'd put his in his frog bank. He had been saving up a long time for a computer. This would speed things up a little.

Mr. Dorfman came into the room. "I'm going for the pizza," he announced. "Any special requests?"

"The usual," said Mrs. Dorfman. "Don't forget some with pepperoni for Robert."

Family Stories

While his dad was out, the rest of Robert's family caught up on family news.

Grandma Judy talked about poor Mrs. Restivo, an old family friend, dying suddenly of a heart attack.

Robert lay on the floor, scratching Huckleberry behind his ears.

"And what do you think about Becky Weinstein getting engaged?" Grandma Judy said, a big smile on her face.

Robert didn't know who Becky Weinstein was. His mom must have known her because she smiled. "Yes," she said. "Isn't it nice?"

Mom reported that her travel agency business was doing really well. Robert wondered why his mom liked her job so much. She made vacation plans for everyone else, but the Dorfmans hardly ever went on family vacations.

Charlie told Grandma Judy about his team winning the hockey championship. He was recounting various football victories when the front door opened.

Whew! That was close. Robert was glad he didn't have to hear Charlie cover every sport he played. He didn't think there was enough time in one day.

"I had an idea on the way home," said Mr. Dorfman, boxes piled in his arms. He kicked the door closed behind him. Huckleberry ran to greet him.

Mr. Dorfman placed the pizza boxes on the coffee table, where Mrs. Dorfman had laid out placemats. "Instead of a regular movie, we can show Grandma Judy the video of our trip to Coney Island."

Robert reached over and grabbed Huckleberry just as the bouncy puppy discovered the food.

"Great!" shouted Charlie. "Grandma Judy, wait'll you see us way up on the roller coaster. If you listen, you can hear Robert scream!"

"Can not!" said Robert, hanging on to Huckleberry. He had not screamed, but he had thought he was going to die. He didn't think you could tell that in the video.

Dad put the tape in the VCR, and they helped themselves to pizza.

Robert shared his slice with Huckleberry.

After the Coney Island video, and one of Robert in his Dracula costume for

Halloween, there was another showing an
old man walking across the yard with a
toddler holding on to his index finger.

"That was Charlie's sixth birthday party," said his mom. "See him over there riding his new bike? And that's Grandpa Aaron, Robert, teaching you to walk."

Robert never knew his grandfather, who died when Robert was just a baby. He was too young to remember the scene in the video.

Grandma Judy got a little teary. "Grandpa liked only pepperoni on his pizza, like you," she told Robert.

"Really?" said Robert. That made him feel better. At least he felt a connection now to the older man in the video.

"It's great to remember old times," Grandma Judy said. She turned to Robert and Charlie. "But you children are young. You are still creating your memories."

Robert yawned. It was getting late, and he had to take Huckleberry out in the yard one more time. The puppy was just about housebroken, but Robert didn't want to take any chances.

He would have to wait until tomorrow to tell Grandma Judy about his project and the protest.

Shocked

On Saturday morning, Robert got dressed quickly.

"C'mon, Huck," he said. He bounced downstairs with the puppy at his heels.

His dad and Charlie weren't down yet. "Hi, Mom. Hi, Grandma Judy," he said.

"Good morning, Robert," said his mom.

"Good morning, handsome," said Grandma Judy.

Robert let Huckleberry out into the yard and sat down at the kitchen table. He poured some Raisin Explosion cereal into his bowl.

"So how are you doing in school?" asked Grandma Judy.

"Gfff," he answered, his mouth full.

"You have a nice teacher?" she asked.

Robert nodded. When he had swallowed, he added, "Mrs. Bernthal. She's really nice. She bought us a snake for our class."

"She bought you a snake?" Grandma Judy made a face.

"She's really great, Grandma. Her name is Sally, and she's green."

"Your teacher is green?"

"No!" Robert laughed. "The snake, Grandma Judy!"

"Boy oh boy oh boy," said Grandma Judy. "School wasn't like that in my day. "

"And you know what else, Grandma Judy?" Robert said. He knew she would like hearing about his endangered animal project and especially about the anti-fur protest.

"Maybe you'd better finish your juice now and tell Grandma Judy on the way," his mom interrupted. "We're going to the mall, and I'd like you to come with us."

"Okay," said Robert, reaching for his glass. "How come?"

Robert often stayed home by himself after school. He had planned on finishing his mask. He still had to paint it and cut out eyeholes.

"Because we may be a while—and Grandma Judy wants to go to Smilin' Jack's for lunch." She smiled. "We thought you'd like to come along."

Smilin' Jack's! Robert looked at Grandma Judy. She grinned. It was his favorite place, and it had become hers, too, when she came to visit.

Robert was the one who first told Grandma Judy about it. He knew she would like the old-fashioned decor of the restaurant. There were comic strips and movie posters on the walls. Old TV commercials, in black and white, played on TVs placed around the room.

Being there made Grandma Judy think of great stories to tell about what it was like in the old days. She once told him how she and her brother had talked their parents into buying many different cereals just to get the prizes they had inside or to save the box tops for bigger prizes.

"We had so much cereal, we could have opened a store!" she had said, laughing.

"There were prizes in your cereal?" Robert had asked.

"Oh my, yes," Grandma Judy had said. "Pins and cards and little figures. We collected them all. And if you saved up enough box tops and sent them in, you could get rings with whistles or secret decoders in them."

Robert wished his cereal had something interesting in it besides raisins. Robert brought his bowl and glass over to the sink and then let Huckleberry in.

They were getting ready to leave. Robert poured puppy food into Huckleberry's bowl and put fresh water in his water dish.

"Good-bye, Huck," he said. "We'll be back soon. Now you be good," he reminded the puppy. He put on his jacket and waited outside.

The garage door opened, and his mom backed the car out of the garage. Grandma Judy was already in the front seat, her seat belt fastened.

Robert climbed into the backseat and
looked at his grandmother in shock.

She was wearing a fur coat!

Public Enemy #1

Robert was so surprised, he didn't know what to say or do. He just sat back as his mom and Grandma Judy chattered away.

As he stared at the fur wrapped around his grandmother, Robert's mind raced. What kind of animal is that, anyway? Does Grandma Judy know how many of them got killed to make that coat? She's the kind of person the anti-fur people hate! What if someone from his class saw him walking next to a fur coat?

"Can I wait in the car?" Robert asked, as they pulled into a spot in the parking lot.

"No, Robert, you may not," said his mom.

Rats! Maybe if he had said "May I" instead of "Can I" his mom would have let him.

As they got out of the car, Robert leaned back in to open the glove compartment. He took out a pair of sunglasses his dad had left there. He put them on.

"Robert, you're being weird," his mom said.

"Oh, let him be," said Grandma Judy. "All the children dress in costumes these days. Haven't you noticed?"

She motioned with her head to a couple of girls passing by. One had on purple striped pants and the other wore earrings that could almost be Christmas tree ornaments.

"I guess so," Robert's mom said, laughing.

Robert walked along way ahead of his mom and his grandmother.

He tried to duck whenever he thought he recognized someone. Once, he thought he

saw Brian Hoberman coming and ducked into a store.

"Robert, why are you going in here?" his mom asked, following him.

Robert slid the sunglasses down on his nose. He was surrounded by half-naked mannequins wearing ladies' underwear! He ran out again.

"Robert, what is the matter with you?" his mom asked, running to catch up to him. Grandma Judy arrived a moment later, panting.

"Is something wrong?" Grandma Judy asked. She sat down on a bench where she could catch her breath.

"No," said Robert. "I . . . I just made a mistake." He held up the glasses. "It must have been these dark glasses."

"Please stay close to us from now on," said his mom. "Grandma Judy doesn't expect to run through the mall."

Robert remained as hidden from sight as possible until they finally left the mall and drove to Smilin' Jack's.

As always, just walking into the restaurant made Robert feel good. Robert read the posters on the walls. One was a movie poster for *The Wizard of Oz*. Another was for *Frankenstein*.

A woman showed them to a booth with an old-fashioned radio in it. You could press a button and hear a snippet from an old radio program.

"Play one, go ahead," Grandma Judy said.

Robert did. A woman's voice came on saying, "McGee, don't open that closet!" Then a man's voice answered, "It's okay, Molly, I just want to get my—" and the next thing you heard was a door opening and a lot of stuff crashing down.

Grandma Judy laughed so hard she had to wipe her eyes. It did sound pretty funny.

"You play one," Robert said to Grandma Judy.

With the press of a button came the sound of hoofbeats and music. A voice told about a masked man.

"That's the *Lone Ranger*," Grandma Judy said. "He had a companion named Tonto who called him 'Kemo Sabe.'"

"You remember that?" asked Robert's mom.

"Sure I do," said Grandma Judy. "I remember them all like it was yesterday. *Mr. Keen, Tracer of Lost Persons*. The *Green Hornet*, where they played that buzzy bee music. . . ."

"You mean the 'Flight of the Bumblebee'?" asked Robert's mom.

"Yes, that's it. And *Ellery Queen*. And *Boston Blackie*: 'Enemy to those who make him an enemy; friend to those who have no friend.'"

Robert enjoyed hearing the bits from the old programs and watching Grandma Judy as she remembered.

"It was exciting," she said. "Every night there was a program about good guys going after bad guys."

"What was your favorite?" asked Robert's mom.

"This I remember very well. It was *The FBI in Peace and War*. They had an announcer who talked about Public Enemy #1. Every week they had another story about one of them and how the FBI tracked him down and put him in jail."

Robert put down his Wimpy Burger, named after a comic-strip character. He was no longer hungry. He imagined another poster on the wall, an FBI wanted poster, and underneath it was the notice: GRANDMA JUDY, PUBLIC ENEMY #1.

Keeping the Secret

That night, Robert tried to write his report, but he had trouble getting started. What could he say about how wrong it was to kill animals for their fur when his own grandmother wore a fur coat!

Huckleberry scratched at his pants leg to get his attention. Robert picked him up.

How could she do it? Grandma Judy loved animals. She even brought a toy for Huckleberry!

"Mom, can I use the phone?" he called down the stairs to his mom.

"Okay," she answered, "but don't stay on too long."

Robert put Huckleberry down and dialed Paul's number. He knew it by heart.

"I have to tell you something," he said. "And you have to promise not to tell. It's a secret."

"Okay," said Paul.

Robert swallowed hard. "My grandmother is a murderer," he said.

"What?" cried Paul. "Get out of here!"

"It's true. She wears a fur coat. The anti-fur people say people who wear fur coats are murderers."

"They also go around spray painting people who wear fur," said Paul.

"Yes, but they're trying to stop people from killing animals," said Robert. "Like those boats that keep hunters from getting close to the baby seals."

"I don't know," said Paul. "It's good that the baby seals are safe, but ruining someone else's property is wrong, no matter why they do it."

"Yeah. You're right," said Robert. "I liked how mad they got about the animals, though. I even wanted to be one of them."

"You don't have to be one of them," said Paul. "You can do something else."

"Like what?" asked Robert.

"I don't know. We'll think of something," said Paul.

"I . . . I feel so funny now around Grandma Judy," Robert confessed. "It's not the same anymore. I used to love her. . . ."

"You don't love your grandma anymore?" Paul sounded shocked.

"I'm trying not to," said Robert, feeling miserable.

"Why?" asked Paul.

"How can I love someone who does something I hate?"

"I don't know," said Paul, "but you've got to. She's your grandmother."

"I have to go," said Robert. "My mom doesn't want me to stay on the phone too long."

"Okay. See you."

That night, Robert dreamed again about Huckleberry being chased. But this time it was Grandma Judy holding the knife.

Good Publicity

Robert, Emily, Vanessa, and Lester were on the floor of Paul's room, where they were all sharing jars of poster paint. Paul sat at his desk, doing his sign in markers.

Emily and Vanessa and Robert had remembered to bring poster board for their signs, but Lester had forgotten. Paul had found a cardboard carton in the basement that Lester was able to tear apart to use for his sign.

Robert looked at his sign. The bright

blue S and T looked pretty good. He made an O, nice and round, then a P.

Robert couldn't help thinking about Grandma Judy as he painted.

He knew the protest was the right thing to do. So why did he feel bad? He guessed it was because he thought he couldn't love Grandma Judy because she did something he didn't like. But that didn't make sense.

Robert stopped painting, right in the middle of a K.

Grandma Judy smoked cigarettes, and he hated that, but he still loved her. Maybe this was like the cigarettes. You could hate something someone does, but that doesn't mean you don't love them.

He went back to his sign.

The protest had grown. Some of the other kids were going, too, if their parents said it was all right. So far Brian, Lester,

Vanessa, Emily, Susanne Lee, Paul, and Robert were planning to go. All they needed now was an adult to go with them.

"I asked my mom," said Paul. "She wasn't sure what she had to do on Saturday, but I think she'll go. She thinks it's a good idea."

"That's great," said Robert. For once, he was glad his mom would be busy. She was taking Grandma Judy into New York to Radio City Music Hall. Grandma Judy loved the Rockettes.

Mrs. Felcher came in. "Popcorn, everyone," she said, looking for a place to set down a big bowl. She moved Paul's books from the top of his bookcase onto his bed and put the bowl there.

Lester got up immediately to grab a handful of popcorn.

"Thanks!" he said, grinning at Mrs. Felcher.

"Oh, those look great," said Mrs. Felcher, looking around the room at the signs.

"Thank you, Mrs. Felcher," said Emily. Her sign, in red letters, read DON'T BE A MURDERER.

Vanessa had painted a picture of a baby seal and her sign, in green, read PLEASE DON'T KILL ME.

"By the way," said Mrs. Felcher, "I'll be able to go with you tomorrow."

"Yay!" yelled Lester, taking more popcorn.

"Double yay!" said Vanessa.

"Cool," said Robert.

"Be sure to tell your parents to call me to let me know it's okay."

"Okay," said Robert.

"We will," said Emily and Vanessa at the same time.

Lester just nodded. His mouth was full of popcorn.

"Great. I'll even carry a sign, if you paint one for me," said Mrs. Felcher.

"I'll do it!" cried Vanessa.

"No, me," said Emily.

"I want to do it!" cried Lester.

Mrs. Felcher laughed. "Well, you can fight over me if you want to, just as long as I have a sign to carry."

Robert got up from the floor. His sign was done. He stepped back to look at it. He hadn't left enough room at the end so he had to squeeze the letters together for the last word. Still, it looked pretty good.

STOP KILLING ANIMALS. TO MAKE FUR COATS

He swished his paintbrush around in the water until it was clean.

When they were all finished and had cleaned up, they picked up their backpacks and went downstairs to wait for Mr. Dorfman, who was going to drive them home.

At the door, Mrs. Felcher reminded them to have their parents call her. "And be ready at ten o'clock. That's when I'll be by to pick you up."

Robert pulled Paul aside.

"I thought about it," he said. "And I know I can love my grandma after all."

"How come?" asked Paul.

"Because I love my grandma, not her coat."

"Cool," said Paul with a smile.

Robert's dad arrived, and the kids shouted their goodbyes as they raced out to the car.

"I wonder if we'll get our names in the newspaper," said Emily as she climbed into the backseat.

"Oh, boy!" shouted Lester Willis, right behind her. "Wouldn't that be great?"

Robert gulped. He didn't think that would be great at all. What if Grandma Judy picked up the newspaper and read about the protest? Or saw a picture of him carrying his sign?

The Protest

The next morning, Robert avoided questions about what he was doing that day. He took Huckleberry out into the yard to play while his mom and dad and Grandma Judy ate bagels for breakfast.

His mom knew where he was going, but Robert asked her not to tell Grandma Judy. He explained why.

"All right, Robert," said his mom, "but I think you'd be better off telling her."

When Paul and his mom honked the horn, Robert brought Huckleberry back into the house. "Bye!" he shouted as he grabbed his mask and ran out the door to the waiting station wagon.

At the mall, kids were assembled in front of Fancy Furs, carrying their signs.

Brian Hoberman's sign read FUR COATS MEAN DEAD ANIMALS.

Abby's sign had a drawing of a cute beaver and I HAVE RIGHTS, TOO underneath it.

Vanessa and Emily presented a sign to Mrs. Felcher that she could carry. "We worked on it together," said Vanessa.

"Read it out loud," said Emily.

Mrs. Felcher read her sign. "'NO FAIR, NO FUR.'" She smiled. "I like it. Thank you, girls."

Robert had to laugh at Lester's sign. It was a big picture of Bugs Bunny that Lester must have copied. In a cartoon balloon over his head it read IS THAT MY RELATIVE YOU'RE WEARING?

"Robert!" said Emily. "What a good idea to wear an animal mask."

Robert didn't tell Emily he had only brought it with him to hide his face if somebody took their picture.

A woman stopped to ask them what they were doing. She squinted at Robert's sign. "What does that mean?" she asked. "Stop killing animals to make fur cots? Who makes fur cots?"

"Coats," said Robert. "Fur *coats*." He heard Vanessa giggle behind him.

"Oh," said the lady. She walked on.

A couple of teenage girls walked by.

"Hey," said one of them. "Good for you."

"Look at his mask!" said the other, pointing to Robert. "What are you supposed to be?" she asked him.

"A clouded leopard," he answered.

The girl laughed and said, "A clowny leopard? What's that?"

Robert started to correct her, but the first girl cracked up and the second one started laughing, too. They walked off together, laughing so hard they were holding their stomachs.

Children stopped to stare at Robert and his classmates marching in a circle with their signs. Their mothers quickly came and pulled them along.

After a while, a man came out of the store.

"What are you doing?" he cried. "Get away from my store. People won't come in, with you hanging around."

"That's the idea," said Emily, waving her sign at the man.

"I'm calling security," the man said, storming inside.

A few minutes later, a man in a uniform came by, asking what they were up to.

"It's a peaceful demonstration," said Mrs. Felcher. "These children are protesting the wearing of fur."

"Do you have a permit?" asked the security guard.

"I don't believe we need one to walk on public property if we're not causing a disturbance," she answered.

The security guard talked into his walkie-talkie. The store owner came out again, pleading with them to leave. The children kept walking quietly back and forth, carrying their signs.

Robert was feeling a little hot and sweaty under his mask and was thinking of taking it off. Just then, a man came at him with a camera.

"Sonny, hold it right there," he said. *Click!*

The photographer moved from Robert to the others.

Whew! That was close. Robert kept the mask on.

The protest went on for two hours before a policeman came up to Mrs. Felcher and told her they would have to leave. She listened to what he had to say and then, with a shrug, told the children they had to go. She led them out of the building.

"Well, children," she said. "You did a magnificent job. I'm sorry you couldn't stay longer, but it seems the mall has a right to ask you to leave. If you want to protest, you have to stay outside the building."

They looked around. The building was huge.

"And that just won't work," she added. "People won't know what you're protesting. I'm proud of you for coming out today to stand up for what you believe in. You can all go home now feeling good about yourselves."

Mrs. Felcher hung out with them until everyone's ride had come. Finally, they were all accounted for. Robert climbed into the station wagon, happy to take off the mask.

It was a good day. Now, if only Grandma Judy didn't find out about it.

Times Change

It was quiet when Robert came downstairs Sunday morning. His mom and dad were still asleep. He let Huckleberry out the back door to the yard and wandered into the living room.

Grandma Judy was reading the entertainment section of the Sunday paper. "Hi," he said, plopping down on the sofa next to her. The first section of the newspaper lay open on the coffee table. Robert strained to see if there was anything there about the protest.

"Hello," said Grandma Judy with a big smile. "And how are you this morning?"

"Fine," he said.

Grandma Judy said, "That's good," and continued to look at the newspaper.

"No, that's not true," said Robert. Grandma Judy lowered the newspaper and looked up.

"What's not true?" she asked. "You're not fine?"

Robert couldn't bear it any longer. Keeping the secret about Grandma Judy's fur coat from his friends had been bad. Keeping his feelings from Grandma Judy was a lot worse.

"Grandma Judy, I have to tell you something."

"Okay. So tell."

And there, on the sofa, still in his pajamas, Robert told his grandmother everything.

"I'm sorry, Grandma Judy," he said as he

finished. His throat almost closed up as he tried not to cry.

"Robert, my love," said Grandma Judy, pulling him to her in a big hug. "You mustn't feel so bad. I understand completely." She stroked his head. "Let me tell you a story." Robert relaxed in Grandma Judy's warm hug.

"From the old days?" he asked.

"Yes, as a matter of fact. From the old days." She smiled and got that look in her eyes that always happened when she talked about Grandpa Aaron.

"It was our 30th wedding anniversary," Grandma Judy said. "Your grandfather, my wonderful Aaron, came home from work with this box. It was a big box. I had no idea what it was. I opened the box. There were roses, lots of roses.

"I took the roses out and pushed the box aside. I was about to get a vase, but Aaron stopped me.

"'No, wait. Look some more,' he said.

"'In the box?' I asked.

"'Where else?' he said. Underneath the tissue paper was a fur coat. It was so soft, so beautiful, I cried.

"'For me?' I asked.

"'Who else?' he said. He was so romantic, your grandfather."

Robert gulped.

Grandma Judy's voice got softer.

"In those days we didn't think so much about animals—maybe we were too busy worrying about ourselves. Now, everything is animal rights, and people rights, and that's good. Times change. And we should be happy they do."

She squeezed him tight. "But my Aaron, he did something beautiful for me with that coat, and I can't forget that."

For a while, they just sat there like that. It was a beautiful story. Robert wished he had known his grandpa Aaron. He also wished Grandpa Aaron had given Grandma Judy jewelry or something and not a fur coat. Nobody got hurt making jewelry. At least, he didn't think they did.

Grandma Judy was warm and smelled like lilacs. He had missed that wonderful flowery smell that was her. "I'm glad you came to see us, Grandma Judy," he told her.

"Even with my fur coat?" she asked, laughing.

Robert smiled. "Yes. Even with your fur coat."

Later, after tossing a ball to Huckleberry in the yard and playing tug-of-war with his rope toy, Robert went up to his room. Huckleberry curled up on the rug while Robert sat at his desk and wrote his report.

Robert felt a lot better now that he had talked to Grandma Judy. But what would he do about the kids in school? Would they understand if he told them about Grandma Judy's fur coat?

The Report

Robert walked into the classroom and stopped short. There were animals sitting where some of the kids should be.

"Your idea was great," said Emily Asher from under an elephant mask. It had big floppy ears and tusks made from paper towel rollers painted white. Brian had on a buffalo mask with black yarn pasted on for the beard and the head. Vanessa's baby seal mask had big sad eyes.

Paul's was the best. His was a big gray whale. The mask had a little hole in the top, and Paul squirted water through a long tube to make it spout like a sperm whale.

"That's cool," said Robert.

"So is yours," said Paul. "Where did you get those whiskers? You didn't have them at the protest."

"From a broom," Robert answered. "I glued them on last night." Paul laughed.

Robert was glad Paul liked his mask. Paul was the best artist he had ever known. He would know how hard it was to paint all those spots to look like little clouds. Robert had taken his time and had been really careful. He only spilled the jar of black paint once. Luckily, it was on the kitchen table, where it was easy to clean up. His mom hadn't even yelled at him for mopping it up with the souvenir dish towel from Atlantic City. She said she had never liked that towel.

When it was Robert's turn to give his report, he spoke loud and clear, so he could be understood through the mask.

"The clouded leopard is very fast," he said, "and a good climber. It can even hang by its back feet from a tree branch."

"No way!" shouted Lester, who never raised his hand before he spoke.

"Way!" said Robert. "It's true. People want its fur to make into coats because it's so unusual," he said. "Now there are only a few left. The clouded leopard is on the endangered list."

Looking around, Robert saw that the kids were moved by his talk. He put down his papers with all his notes. He took off his mask and stood up straight.

"My grandma wears a fur coat," he said. Several kids gasped. Robert swallowed hard.

"She's not a bad person," he said. "She's nice and she's funny. A long time ago, people didn't think about animal rights the way they do now. But times change," said Robert, "and we know better now."

Robert's voice was a little shaky. He cleared his throat.

"I think we have to help the animals on our planet, not kill them. It's up to us to protect them." He collected his papers and took his seat.

"That was a very good report, Robert," said Mrs. Bernthal. "It shows you did your research and learned all about your subject." She turned from Robert to face the whole class.

"I heard about your protest at the mall on Saturday," she said. "The fact that you did something about what you learned is admirable."

Admirable. That meant Mrs. Bernthal admired them! She turned to look at Robert again.

His cheeks felt warm.

He wished he still had the mask on so nobody could see him blushing.

Hello Again

"**R**oll over!"
 Huckleberry's tiny tail wagged as he tumbled over at Robert's command. They were just finishing a show of tricks for Grandma Judy.

"Such a smart puppy," she said. "Did you teach him all these tricks, Robert?"

Robert nodded. He was glad that Huckleberry did his newest trick perfectly for Grandma Judy.

Grandma Judy scooped up the puppy. "I'm going to miss you, young fellow," she said, nuzzling the dog's neck.

Grandma Judy's visit was coming to an end. Robert's dad was about to drive her to the airport. He stood there with her luggage as Mrs. Dorfman got Grandma Judy's coat.

"It's time to say good-bye," she said, putting Huckleberry down, "until we say hello again." She wrapped her arms around Charlie and then Robert. "I like to think of it that way so I don't have to dwell on the good-bye part."

"I love you, Grandma Judy," said Robert. "I'm sorry about the fur coat."

Grandma Judy stepped back and looked at him. "Robert, my love, don't think another minute about it," she said. "I am proud that you are such a caring person. I feel safe that you will be in charge of the world one day."

He smiled at the thought of being in charge of anything besides the class library and the class pet and Huckleberry. Wow! He didn't realize until just then that he was responsible for so much!

Mrs. Dorfman helped her mother into her coat.

"Besides," added Grandma Judy, "I'm thinking—it's time to retire this old coat."

"Really?" said Robert.

"Yes," she replied. "Times change. Fur is not in fashion anymore. I have to get

with it and buy myself a new modern coat. What do you think of a red one?"

Robert gave her a big hug, smelling her lilac perfume once more.

"Red would be perfect," he told her.